TOTAL
DARKNESS

Rich Harris

For Steph. X

<u>I really fell for you.</u>

Falling in love can be easy.
It's the getting back up again when it ends that's the tricky bit.

This ones a howler.

He's not so much a 'lone-wolf', but more a 'lonely- wolf'.

<u>Angel in disguise.</u>

BEWARE!

Caucasian male
Youthful, cherub-like looks
Distinctive 'angel wings'
Known to carry bladed weapons
Reports of stabbing victims in the heart

Do not approach this man. If you see him, call the authorities.

Crazy.

Depression. It's just mental.

Love bubble.

There's nothing greater you will see
Than those three dots, that basically
Mean someone thinks enough of you
To type a text and send it through

Of all the ways to manifest
A love note, I can now attest
That it shall be greatly received
My heart it shall not be deceived

I wonder what his text will say
I hope it's more than 'How's your day'
It's surely plain for all to see
Why else would he be texting me?

Initially I texted first
I sat down and composed my verse
I poured my love into that note
I think it worked; I shall not gloat

I've watched each day and week pass by
Just aching for his quick reply
And though waiting can be a bore
Some things are just worth waiting for

Oh hang on now, its coming through,
My love story is coming true!
Oh dear, that's not what I expected
It seems my love has been rejected

He said he didn't know my name
And wasn't keen to play my game
He signed it off – this part is sore
'Pls do not txt me anymore'

I cannot lie, I am defeated
And his number, I deleted
These days I sit here, patiently
For those three dots to come to me.

<u>He who cares, wins.</u>

'*If nobody else is ever going to love me*', he thought, '*then neither will I.*'

<u>A walk in the park.</u>

Unlovable,
unwanted,
undesired you suppose
but you've crushed so many flowers
on your quest to find a rose
open-minded, open-thinking,
open-hearted if you please;
if you want to find the forest
reconsider all the trees.

A chemical in balance.

It was billed as entertaining
And it twinkled just like glitter
But my head was topsy-turvy;
My emotions in the shitter
So I threw away my ticket
And decided not to ride
See you later, off you go now
I'll just stay here with my pride.

<u>Higher and higher.</u>

The greatest high of all, is not being high at all.

Into me see.

Empty
Uninspired
Broken
Tired
Unenthused
Jaded
Underused
Faded
Crushed
Weak
Hopeful
Bleak

This list is not exhaustive, although it is an exhausting list.

Love fool.

A fool in love will fall in love.

<u>No today Satan, not today.</u>

Empty threats are
a darkening sky
You summon a storm but it seems to stay dry
By walking through clouds you're certain you're right
Miraculous, though
it's still sunny and bright.

Heart; felt.

Be willing to try
But beware, you may fall
To get to my heart
You must first scale a wall
And if you succeed
Then I'm pleased that you tried
But defeat lies ahead;
It's still locked from inside.

Love. It's a piece of cake.

Whisper softly in my ear,
Three little words I long to hear,
The words for which my heart does ache
Whisper them softly; 'Slice. Of. Cake'.

Soho.

The night hangs on you like a stain,
your streets are heavy, under rain
They shine like mirrors you've collected,
where filthy, neon love's reflected

Where strangers march, no time to spare,
some place to be, no chance to care
An angry, hungry, tired nation
trudge from Tottenham Court Road Station

A punctured sky has long begun,
with cranes, all reaching for the sun
They drag up London by its scruff
and build it up all strong and tough

When night drips down like murky ink,
it welcomes every whim and kink
A seedy backdrop filled with lust
and grabbing hands tug at your trust

I must be careful where I tread;
a misplaced step may leave me dead
Those landmines scattered here and there,
explosions come from everywhere

And church bells, oh, you never cease;
a constant chime of disbelief
Sunday was a day of rest
but now, you've put that to the test

You know just how to find my tears;
we've been together many years
Your blackened heart is cruel and strong
but this is where I do belong.

I forgot my dream.

Chase your dream but keep in mind
it may keep running faster,
There comes a time to stop
before it all ends in disaster.

In Tense

If your heart only sees the past,
How will you ever recognise the future?

<u>Survival.</u>

- · Keys
- · Wallet
- · Phone
- · Oyster card
- · Deflector shield

<u>Do you miss me?</u>

I miss who I used to be.

<u>My favourite.</u>

Fortune favours the bold, but heartache favours the lonely.

The cards I've been dealt.

My life may be a deck of cards,
or a losing hand a poker;
I've never had a pair of hearts
and I always find the joker.

<u>No place like home.</u>

You can live in the biggest house in the world
And fill it with things you don't need
But if you have nobody to share it all with
Such a lonely, sad life you will lead

Stormy weather.

Occasionally your name floats into my mind, like a rain cloud darkening a sunny day.

<u>'The end'.</u>

We all need a love-story, even when it's nothing more than fiction.

CTRL + DEL

I saw your name in my contacts list
And I thought DO NOT REPEAT
So I wiped my eyes,
Accepted goodbyes,
Then filed you under DELETE

Last chance.

It slipped right through your fingers;
You watched it float away
Lightning will not strike here twice –
Perhaps it's best that way.

S.L.H.

It hasn't stopped raining all day
It's been overcast, cloudy and grey
But the sun in the sky.
Says it's pleasant and dry
Guess my heart sees it differently, hey?

<u>Ready, aim, fire.</u>

Loaded words fly like bullets.
Dodge carefully and they'll miss.
Take a hit though, and you will bleed forever.

Tempted?

Lead me not into temptation.
I've been before and honestly, they gave me a loyalty card.

Lost for words.

I tried to write
a poem here,
but had to walk away,
that's the thing;
when you feel loss there's just
no words to say.

If it's not broken....

Sometimes hearts get 'broken'
By a lover who pretends,
But a heart that breaks from death and loss
Is a heart that never mends.

<u>The son doesn't always shine.</u>

Keep telling yourself 'you did all that you could',
You can lie to yourself, and pretend
But it wasn't enough,
Don't blame me when it's rough;
Now regret seems to be your best friend.

Regret-fool.

Love while you can
Lest not we forget
For a life is no life
When it's lived in regret

<u>Gotcha.</u>

Love conquers fool.

Slow burner.

Before you go and fall in love
Here's something to remember;
A spark is great (but may not last)
So choose a burning ember.

Back to the Grind.

I'm not saying he's needy and desperately lonely, but his Grindr profile headline says:

'Looking to be gang-hugged'.

Sweet dreams are made of this.

Zopiclone
Triazolam
Temazepam
Xanax
Nitrazepam
…..

<u>Its that ol' devil.....</u>

The devil makes work for idle hearts.

Life is a drag.

Some people deserve a chance
To leap off from their shelf
But how you gonna love someone
If you can't even love yourself?

Can I get an amen up in here?

<u>Prick me!</u>

Imagine this; your heart inflates if love should quench your thirst,
But as usual – it only takes 'one prick' for it to burst.

Happy birthday.

I don't want any gifts or cards,
There's reason for my gloom,
A flame, (not from my birthday cake),
Extinguished much too soon.

Wakey-wakey!

Boyfriend hunting is a bit like breakfast cereal.
I tend to go for nutty ones, fruit loops and of course, flakes.

Twisting my sobriety

Tell me, what's your drug of choice
We're all allowed a vice
Try a little taster first
Maybe you'll try it twice?

Tell me, what's your drug of choice
I bet you like a drink?
A pint, a shot, a glass or two
Acceptable, don't you think?

Tell me, what's your drug of choice
You like to chase a line?
Cavort and snort, but keep it short
I'm sure they think it's fine

Tell me, what's your drug of choice
Oh, you like to smoke weed
That's commonplace these days I think
At least, it seems agreed

Tell me what's your drug of choice
You passing round the pipe?
That dirty bowl, that empty soul
Now, is it worth the hype?

Tell me, what's your drug of choice
You shoot up with a pin?
A vein in vain, hides all the pain
No wonder you fit in

Tell me, what's your drug of choice
It may set you apart
For you just want to fall in love
To mend your broken heart

Tell me, what's your drug of choice
You must know what I mean
However you reach giddy heights
You're far from fucking clean.

Say 'cheese'.

His Instagram posts were not so much a celebrated tapestry of his life...,
more a chronicled descent into his current state of misery.

Hey Siri.

He spent a whole day staring into his phone
Desperately hunting on Grindr
He missed breakfast, lunch, dinner
Grew terribly thinner
He should have set a reminder

Paneful.

Love is the window I look through to see other people's happiness.

Sonnet.

How do I hate me, let me count the ways;

1- Monday
2- Tuesday
3- Wednesday
4- Thursday
5- Friday
6- Saturday
7- Sunday

<u>Taxi for one.</u>

Had enough?
Feel like you've outstayed your welcome?
Leaving the party early?

Then choose **Koffin Kars.**

'The best drive ever, even if it is just to the end of the road'.

<u>Oh God.</u>

Dear God.

Hi. Hope you're well

Sorry to bother you, again. I know you're probably very busy but I've not
yet heard back from you and I just wondered if you could at least confirm
receipt of my prayers?
I think in total there's around 7,042.

Many thanks. Rich.

PS – might be worth checking SPAM/JUNK?

Nothing. Nowhere. No-one.

Tell me; what am I going to do?
Nothing. Stay in bed 'til 2.

Tell me; where am I going to go?
Nowhere. That's the place I know.

Tell me; who am I going to see?
No-one. Always only me.

Tell me; isn't it always the same?
Nothing. Nowhere. No-one.

<u>Cranked.</u>

Life is better in stereo.

<u>Orange.</u>

The future's bright. The future's slate grey.

Life imitating heart.

Twice I've had a brush with love
And twice, a brush with death
My heart remains a steady grey;
There is no colour left.

Bye Felicia!

He packed in the rat-race and swapped it for more of a mole-stroll.

OOO.

What's important in your life,
Is it bricks and mortar?
Or is it laying on white sands,
Caressed by azure waters?
The boardroom?
Just a bored-room
And the desk is still a pest
But my out of office sunset
Is the place I choose to rest.

Banking on it.

They wonder why he sits alone
And why he's so forlorn;
No love interest –
And what says that best
Is a heart that's overdrawn.

<u>Free for all.</u>

The best things in life are 'we'.

Alterations needed.

If your heart is on your sleeve
Expect to see some creases
But worse than those
While it's exposed
It may get ripped to pieces.

It's a date.

Dates; the last bastion of public humiliation. But with cocktails.

Sweet things are bad for you.

I had hoped that these days and being in my forties, my taste in men
would have gotten better?

It's only gotten bitter.

<u>All ways.</u>

I know that you are missing me
Perhaps you always will
Perhaps that 'missing feeling' never strays
But instead of only missing me with sadness, try instead
To remember with a smile, our special days

I know that you are struggling
And fighting through each day
And at times you feel the clouds will never break
But tomorrow is for you to live your life, and live you must!
Life's a gift, don't waste a minute, it won't wait

I know your hearts are broken now
My heart is broken too
But maybe they don't have to break forever?
If you use the love we've shared, some broken bits might get repaired
And that just proves the love we had keeps us together.
Always.

Heart; burn.

After you strike up a match
You might get lost in games
Passion is an angry fuel
Our hearts now burn in flames

Trumped.

Trumpty Dumpty
Is building a wall
But borrows from Peter
Just to pay Paul
His towers are high
But his ego is taller
And his small orange hands
Just get smaller and smaller.

Fermé.

Im open to love but every time I went there, it was closed.

<u>Accepting rainbows.</u>

My sister is my brother
My brother is my sister
My father – she is gorgeous
My mother – such a mister
My children, well, they're beautiful
They dance around details;
My daughter plays with action-man
My son; he paints his nails
My friends each have a colour
Our religions can't compare
My arms, they welcome everyone
I hope to see you there.

<u>Is that it?</u>

He gets laid weekly.

Very weakly.

<u>Now, now.</u>

Hold that thought, that one right there
Don't let it vanish into air
Yesterday won't meet your need;
Tomorrow isn't guaranteed.

I heart London.

London, when I met you you,
how I loved you from the start
But I leave with broken memories
and fragments of a heart.

<u>Fuck up.</u>

When it comes to sex and relationships, I'm an aggressive stop.

<u>End of message.</u>

I'm not saying he has intimacy issues, but the most affectionate he ever gets is via WhatsApp.

Apply within.

I've filled out application forms –
lots more than I expected,
but the vacancy of LOVE remains;
Each form has been rejected.

Constant.

Dive into the silent lake,
Sleep awaits you, never wake,
Those days from which you felt you lack,
Are never, ever coming back.

Chat snapped.

Many times I find myself
Spiralling off kilter
So before they ask
On goes the mask;
Life's better with a filter.

Other titles from Rich Harris are available on WWW.AMAZON.CO.UK as paperback and Kindle editions:

'DARK'
'DARKER'

(And his collaborative work with Mike Harrison):

'The BIG(ish) Book of (somewhat) Hilarious Poems'

Twitter: @richie_rich77

Lightning Source UK Ltd.
Milton Keynes UK
UKHW022007170619
344563UK00020B/785/P